SCHOOL DAYS

The Little House
Chapter Book Collection

The Adventures of Laura & Jack
Pioneer Sisters
Animal Adventures
School Days
Laura & Nellie
Christmas Stories

SCHOOL DAYS

ADAPTED FROM THE **LITTLE HOUSE** BOOKS BY

Laura Ingalls Wilder

Illustrated by Ji-Hyuk Kim

An Imprint of HarperCollins*Publishers*

Adaptation by Melissa Peterson

Little House® is a trademark of HarperCollins Publishers Inc.

School Days
Text adapted from *The Long Winter*, copyright 1940, 1968, Little House Heritage Trust; *On the Banks of Plum Creek*, copyright 1937, 1965, Little House Heritage Trust.
Illustrations by Ji-Hyuk Kim
 For information address HarperCollins Children's Books, a division of HarperCollins Publishers, 195 Broadway, New York, NY 10007.
www.littlehousebooks.com

Library of Congress Control Number: 2017949559
ISBN 978-0-06-237711-1

Typography by Jenna Stempel
17 18 19 20 21 BVG 10 9 8 7 6 5 4 3 2 1

❖

Revised edition, 2017

Contents

CHAPTER 1
GOING TO SCHOOL

Laura and Mary were sisters. They had a baby sister named Carrie, and a Ma and a Pa.

One day Ma said, "Now we're nicely settled and only two and a half miles from town, you can go to school."

Laura and Mary looked at each other. School?

The more Laura thought about it, the more she didn't want to go. There was so much to do right there at home, on the banks of Plum Creek.

"Oh, Ma, do I have to?" she asked.

Ma said that a little girls who are almost eight years old should be learning to read instead of running wild.

"But I can read, Ma," Laura said. "Listen!"

She picked up one of Ma's books. It was called *Millbank*. It was a fat book with small print. She read, "The doors and windows of Millbank were closed. Crepe streamed from the doorknob—"

"Oh, Laura," Ma said, "you are not reading. You are only reciting what you've heard me read to Pa so often. Besides, there are other things to learn—spelling and writing and arithmetic."

And that was that. Laura and Mary would start school on Monday morning.

Laura bounded out of the house. She almost ran into Pa, who was hammering something just outside the door.

"Oops!" said Pa. "Nearly hit you that time, flutterbudget!"

"What are you doing, Pa?"

"Making a fish-trap," said Pa. "Want to help me?"

Laura handed Pa nails one by one. He was building a sort of box with no lid. Pa left wide cracks between the strips of wood.

"How will that catch fish?" Laura asked. "If you put it in the creek they will swim in through the cracks, but they will swim right out again."

"You wait and see," said Pa.

Pa led the way to a steep place in the creek bank. There was a waterfall there. The water crashed and splashed over the edge. Laura

helped Pa set the fish-trap right underneath the waterfall, where the water would pour right into it.

"You see, Laura," said Pa. "The fish will come over the falls into the trap. The little ones will go out through the cracks, but the big ones can't. They'll have to stay swimming in the box till I come and take them out."

At that very minute a big fish splashed over the falls. Laura squealed. "Look, Pa!" she shouted.

Pa grabbed the fish and lifted him out. The fish flopped back and forth in his hands. Laura almost fell into the waterfall. They looked at that silvery fish. Then Pa dropped him back into the trap.

"Oh, Pa, can't we please stay and catch enough fish for supper?" Laura asked.

"I've got to get to work on a barn, Laura," said Pa. "And plow the garden and dig a well and—" He looked at Laura. "Well, little half-pint," he said, "maybe it won't take long."

He sat on his heels. Laura sat on hers and they waited. The creek poured and splashed. It was always the same and always changing. Laura could have watched it forever. The sun danced on the water and lay warm on Laura's neck. It shone on Pa's dark hair.

"Oh, Pa," Laura said, "do I have to go to school?"

"You will like school," said Pa.

"I like it better here," Laura said.

"I know, little half-pint," said Pa. "But it isn't everybody that gets a chance to learn to read and write. Your Ma was a schoolteacher when we met, and when she came West with me I promised that our girls would have a chance to get book learning. You're almost eight years old now, and Mary is going on nine. It's time you began." He smiled at her across the water. "Be thankful you've got the chance, Laura."

"Yes, Pa," Laura sighed.

Just then another big fish came over the falls. And before Pa could catch it there came another!

Laura watched the silvery fish splash in the glittering water. How could she possibly like school better than this?

CHAPTER 2
THE FIRST DAY

Monday morning came. Mary and Laura put on their Sunday dresses. Mary's was a blue-flowered calico and Laura's was red sprigged.

Ma braided their hair and tied the ends with thread. They could not wear their Sunday hair ribbons because they might lose them. But their sunbonnets were freshly washed and ironed.

Then Ma took Laura and Mary into the

bedroom. She took three books out of a special box.

"I am giving you these books for your very own, Mary and Laura," she said. "I know you will take care of them and study them faithfully."

"Yes, Ma," they said. They looked at the books. One was a speller, one was a reader, and one was an arithmetic. They were the very same books Ma had used when she was a little girl.

Ma gave the books to Mary to carry. She gave Laura a little tin pail with their lunch in it.

"Good-bye," she said. "Be good girls."

Mary and Laura walked to the creek. Jack, their bulldog, followed them. Laura stopped to pet him good-bye. Then she and Mary waded across the creek, careful not to splash their clean dresses.

They walked quietly across the green prairie, following a dusty wagon track. Pa had said that town was only two and a half miles away. The road would take them to it. They'd know they were in town when they came to a house.

Laura watched a prairie hen cluck along in front of its tiny peeping chicks. Funny birds called snipes ran through the grass on their long, thin legs. She saw a rabbit standing on its hind legs, its long ears twitching. It stared at her with round eyes.

"For pity's sake, Laura," Mary said, "keep your sunbonnet on! What will the town girls think of us?"

"I don't care!" Laura said loudly and bravely.

"You do, too!" said Mary.

"I don't either!" said Laura.

"You do!"

"I don't!"

"You're just as scared of town as I am," said Mary.

Laura did not answer. After a while she pulled her sunbonnet back over her head.

"Anyway," said Mary, "there's two of us."

They went on and on. After a long time they saw town. It looked like small blocks of wood on the prairie. It got closer and closer. Soon Laura could see smoke rising from the buildings.

Laura and Mary reached the town. They passed a store and a blacksmith shop. More stores. Some houses. Off in once direction came a jumble of children's voices.

"Come on," Mary said. "It's the school where we hear the hollering. Pa said we would hear it."

Laura wanted to turn around and run all the way home, but she and Mary walked slowly toward the jumble of voices. They passed the lumberyard, and there in front of them was the schoolhouse.

CHAPTER 3
P-A-T, PAT

The schoolhouse was at the end of a long, dusty path. Boys and girls stood in the yard in front of it. They were talking and laughing in a tangle of noise.

Slowly Laura walked toward them. Mary came along behind her. All the girls and boys stopped talking and stared at them.

Laura kept on going. She walked nearer and nearer to all those staring eyes. Suddenly, without meaning to, she shouted, "You all sounded just like a flock of prairie chickens!"

"Laura!" Mary gasped. The boys and girls were surprised.

But they were not as surprised as Laura. She felt ashamed. What had made her say such a thing?

Then a boy with red hair and freckles yelled, "Snipes yourselves! Snipes! Long-legged snipes!"

Laura wanted to sink into the ground. Her dress was too short. It was much shorter than the town girls' dresses. So was Mary's. Their bare legs sticking out did look long and spindly, like snipes' legs.

"Snipes!" yelled the boy. All the boys were pointing and yelling. "Snipes! Snipes!"

Then a red-headed girl began to push the boys. "Shut up!" she said. "You make too much noise! Shut up, Sandy," she said to the red-headed boy. He shut up.

The girl walked up to Laura. "My name is Christy Kennedy," she said. "And that horrid boy is my brother Sandy. But he doesn't mean any harm. What's your name?"

Her red hair was braided so tightly that the braids were stiff. Her eyes were dark blue. Her sunbonnet hung down her back.

"Is that your sister?" she said. "Those are my sisters."

She pointed to some big girls who were talking to Mary. "The big one's Nettie, and the black-haired one's Cassie, and then there's Donald and me and Sandy. How many brothers and sisters do you have?"

"Two," Laura said. "That's Mary, and Carrie's the baby. And we have a bulldog named Jack. We live on Plum Creek. Where do you live?"

"Does your Pa drive two bay horses with black manes and tails?" Christy asked.

"Yes," Laura said.

"He comes by our house. So you came by it, too," said Christy. "It's the house before you come to Beadle's store and the blacksmith shop. Miss Eva Beadle's our teacher."

Christy pointed at a girl with long yellow curls. "That's Nellie Oleson," she said.

Nellie Oleson was very pretty. She had two big blue bows in her curly yellow hair. Her dress was white with little blue flowers. And she wore shoes.

Nellie Oleson looked at Laura. She looked at Mary. Then she wrinkled up her nose.

"Hmm!" she said. "Country girls!"

Before anyone else could say anything, a bell rang. A young lady stood in the school-house doorway. She was swinging the bell in her hand.

Laura thought she was beautiful. Her brown hair was frizzed in bangs over her brown eyes. Buttons sparkled down the front of her dress. Her face was sweet and her smile was lovely.

All the boys and girls hurried past the beautiful young lady into the schoolhouse.

She laid her hand on Laura's shoulder. "You're a new little girl, aren't you?" she asked.

"Yes, ma'am," said Laura.

"And this is your sister?" Teacher asked, smiling at Mary.

"Yes, ma'am," said Mary.

"Then come with me," said Teacher, "and I'll write your names in my book."

Laura and Mary followed Teacher into the schoolhouse. The school was one big room. Long benches stood one behind another down the middle of the room. Each bench had a back. Two shelves stuck out from the back, over the bench behind.

These were the students' desks.

Teacher took Laura and Mary up to her desk. She asked them their names and how old they were. Laura stood still as a statue and looked around the room.

There was a broom in one corner and a water-pail by the door. Behind Teacher's desk part of the wall was painted black. Under it was a little shelf. Some kind of short, white sticks lay on the shelf. Next to them was a block of wood half-covered with wool. Laura wondered what those things were.

Mary showed Teacher how much she could read and spell. But Laura looked at Ma's book and shook her head. She could not read. She was not even sure of all the letters.

"Well," said Teacher, "you can begin at the beginning, Laura. And Mary can study farther on. Have you a slate?"

They did not have a slate.

"I will lend you mine," Teacher said. "You cannot learn to write without a slate."

She lifted up the top of her desk. Inside Laura could see books and a ruler and a slate. Teacher took out the slate and gave it to Mary.

Laura and Mary sat side by side on a bench. Mary's feet rested on the floor, but Laura's dangled. The dangling made her legs tired.

They held their speller open on the board shelf in front of them. Laura studied at the front of the book and Mary studied farther on. The pages in between stood straight up.

Laura was the only student who couldn't read yet. That meant she was a whole class by herself. Sometimes Teacher called Laura to her desk and helped her read letters. By noontime on that first day, Laura was able to read C-A-T, cat.

Suddenly she remembered something

she'd seen at home. Written on Ma's iron cookstove were the letters P-A-T. Pa had said they spelled Pat.

"P-A-T, Pat!" she said.

Teacher was surprised.

"R-A-T, rat!" said Teacher. "M-A-T, mat!"

Laura was reading! She could read the whole first row in the speller now.

At noon all the other children and Teacher went home to dinner. Laura and Mary took their pail and sat in the grass to eat their bread and butter.

"I like school," Mary said.

"So do I," said Laura. "Only it makes my legs tired."

CHAPTER 4
THE SLATE PENCIL

Jack was waiting to meet them at the creek that night. At supper they told Pa and Ma all about school.

When they said they were using Teacher's slate, Pa shook his head.

Next morning he gave Mary a silver coin to buy a slate. Ma tied the money in a handkerchief and pinned it inside Mary's pocket.

Mary kept a hand on her pocket all the way to school. Laura swung the dinner-pail and hippety-hopped like the rabbits they passed. The wind was blowing and the sky was clear and blue.

In town, they climbed the steps to Mr. Oleson's store. Pa had said to buy the slate there.

Inside the store was a long counter. The wall behind it was covered with shelves. They were full of tin pans and pots and lamps and lanterns. There were rolls of colored cloth for making clothes. There were nails and wire and hammers and saws for sale.

On the floor was a barrel of molasses and a keg of pickles. Laura saw two tall wooden pails filled with Christmas candy.

Suddenly the back door of the store burst open. Nellie Oleson and her little brother, Willie, came bouncing in.

Nellie wrinkled her nose at Laura and Mary.

"Yah! Yah! Long-legged snipes!" called Willie.

"Shut up, Willie," said Mr. Oleson. But Willie did not shut up.

"Snipes! Snipes!"

Nellie flounced past Mary and Laura. She dug her hands into a pail of candy. Willie dug into the other pail. They grabbed all the candy they could hold and crammed it into their mouths. They didn't offer Mary and Laura a single piece.

"Nellie!" said Mr. Oleson. "You and Willie go right back out of here!"

But Nellie and Willie went on gobbling candy and staring at Mary and Laura.

Mary gave Mr. Oleson the money. He handed her a slate. "You'll want a slate pencil, too," he said. "Here it is. One penny."

"They haven't got a penny," Nellie said.

"Well, take it along, and tell your Pa to

give me the penny next time he comes to town," said Mr. Oleson.

But Mary said, "No, sir. Thank you." She and Laura turned around and walked out of the store.

At the door Laura looked back. Nellie made a face at her. Nellie's tongue was streaked red and green from the candy.

"My goodness!" said Mary. "I couldn't be as mean as that Nellie Oleson."

They looked at their slate's smooth grey surface. It had a smooth wooden frame. It was a handsome slate.

But they must have a slate pencil.

They hated to tell Pa they must have another penny. He had already spent so much for the slate.

Mary and Laura walked along soberly. Suddenly Laura remembered their Christmas pennies. One year, back in Indian Territory, they had each found a penny in their Christmas stockings.

They only needed one slate pencil. They decided that Mary would spend her penny for the pencil. After that she would own half of Laura's penny.

Next morning they bought the pencil. But not from Mr. Oleson. They bought it at Mr. Beadle's store, where Teacher lived. And that morning they got to walk to school with Teacher.

CHAPTER 5
UNCLE JOHN

All through the long, hot weeks they went to school. Every day they liked it more.

They liked reading, writing, and arithmetic. They liked the spelling contest on Friday afternoons.

Most of all Laura loved recess. The boys played games on one side of the schoolhouse. The big girls, like Mary, sat ladylike on the steps. And the little girls rushed out into the sun and the wind to pick wildflowers and play games.

Every day they girls played ring-around-a-rosy, because Nellie Oleson said to. They got tired of it, but they always played it.

One day, before Nellie could say anything, Laura cried out, "Let's play Uncle John!"

"Let's! Let's!" the girls said, taking hold of one another's hands.

But Nellie grabbed Laura's long braids in both hands and jerked, hard. Laura was pulled flat on the ground.

"I want to play ring-around-a-rosy!" shouted Nellie.

Laura jumped up. She was boiling mad. Her hand flashed out to slap Nellie.

She stopped it just in time. Pa said she must never strike anybody.

"Come on, Laura," said Christy, holding out her hand. Laura's face felt hot and she

could hardly see, but she took Christy's hand.

The girls made a circle around Nellie. That was how you played ring around-a-rosy. Nellie tossed her curls because she'd gotten her own way.

Then Christy began singing, and all the others joined in:

"Uncle John is sick abed.
What shall we send him?"

"No! No!" Nellie screamed. "Ring-around-a-rosy! Or I won't play!" She broke through the ring.

No one went after her.

"All right," said Christy. "You get in the middle, Maud," They started over.

"Uncle John is sick abed.
What shall we send him?

A piece of pie, a piece of cake,
Apple and dumpling!
What shall we send it in?
A golden saucer.
Who shall we send it by?
The governor's daughter.
If the governor's daughter ain't at home,
Who shall we send it by?"

Then all the girls shouted,

"By Laura Ingalls!"

Laura stepped into the middle of the ring and her friends went dancing around her.

CHAPTER 6
ANOTHER FIRST DAY

Laura tossed and turned in her bed. She couldn't sleep. Tomorrow she would go to a new school, where she didn't know anyone.

Even though she was older now, and she liked school, it was scary. Her family had moved from Minnesota to the Dakota Territory, and Laura didn't know anyone in town.

This time Carrie would walk beside her. Carrie wasn't the baby of the family anymore. Little Grace was three years old. Laura was thirteen now, and Carrie was ten. For the past year they had lived far from any school, but Ma had taught them at home.

Mary had kept up her studies, too. But she would not be going to school with Laura and Carrie. Mary had caught scarlet fever and the fever had left her blind.

Mary could no longer see, but she still did arithmetic and history lessons in her head. Some day she hoped to go to a college for the blind. But that was a long time off.

Suddenly Laura woke. She must have dozed off at last. It was morning. She heard steps going by in the street below.

For the first time in Laura's life, she lived in a town. Pa had a farm out on the prairie, but they had all moved into town for the winter. Pa had heard that this winter was going to be long and cold and hard.

Laura could hear the sounds of the town

waking up. Storekeepers were opening their stores. It was time to get ready for school.

At breakfast Ma said, "Now Laura and Carrie, there's no cause to worry. I'm sure you can keep up with your classes."

Laura and Carrie looked at Ma in surprise. They knew they'd keep up all right. Ma had taught them well. After all, she had been a schoolteacher once. That wasn't what they were worried about.

But they only said, "Yes, Ma."

They hurried through their morning chores. Laura swept the bedroom floor. Then she and Carrie put on their warm winter dresses and braided their hair. They tied on their Sunday hair ribbons.

Carrie began to button her shoes with nervous hands.

"Hurry up, girls!" Ma called.

Carrie gasped. She'd jerked too hard and a

button had popped off her shoe. The button rolled across the floor and fell down a crack.

"Oh, it's gone!" Carrie cried. She was desperate. She could not go to school with a gap in her shoe. It would look too awful.

But downstairs, Ma had heard the button fall. It has fallen right through the ceiling to the room below. Ma found the button and sewed it on again.

"You look very nice," Ma said, smiling.

Laura and Carrie put on their coats and hoods. They picked up their schoolbooks and went out onto Main Street.

Carrie took Laura's hand. It helped Laura to know that Carrie was even more scared than she was.

It seemed a long, long way to the schoolhouse. The school was at the end of town, out on the open prairie. There were no other buildings nearby.

Laura and Carrie came nearer and nearer. In front of the schoolhouse strange boys were playing ball. Two girls stood near the doorway.

Laura could hardly breathe. She always felt shy around strangers.

Then suddenly Laura saw one of the boys jump into the air and catch the ball. He was tall and quick. He moved like a cat. When he saw Laura, a flashing grin lit up his face. He threw the ball to her.

Before Laura could think, she leapt into the air and caught the ball.

A great shout went up from the other boys. "Hey, Cap!" they yelled. "Girls don't play ball!"

"I didn't think she'd catch it," Cap answered.

"I don't want to play," Laura said. She threw back the ball.

But Cap shouted, "She's as good as any of us!" He called to Laura, "Come on and play!" He turned to the other girls. "Come on, Mary Power and Minnie! You play with us, too!"

But Laura picked up the books she had dropped and took Carrie's hand again. They went to stand near the other girls.

Laura felt terribly ashamed. What must those girls think of her? They would not play ball with boys, she was sure.

"I'm Mary Power," said the tall girl. She had dark hair and a blue dress. It was longer than Laura's dress. With her hair twisted into a knot at the back of her head, she looked almost grown up.

"And this is Minnie Johnson," said Mary Power. Minnie was thin and fair and pale.

"I'm Laura Ingalls," Laura said, "and this is my little sister, Carrie."

Mary Power smiled. Laura smiled back.

She made up her mind that she would twist up her own hair tomorrow. And she'd ask Ma to make her next dress as long as Mary Power's.

"That was Cap Garland who threw you the ball," said Mary Power.

There was no time to say anything more. The teacher came to the door and rang a bell.

The day had begun.

CHAPTER 7
THE NEW SCHOOL

The schoolroom was so new and shining that Laura felt shy again. Carrie stood close beside her. There was a little entryway with nails to hang their coats on. In a corner were a broom and water pail, just like in the little schoolhouse back in Minnesota.

But here the desks weren't just benches with shelves nailed to the back. They were real desks made of smooth, shiny wood. They had black iron feet. The desktops had slots to

hold pencils. Underneath each seat was a shelf for your books and slate.

There were twelve of these desks in rows up each side of the room. In the middle of the room was a big stove. Four more desks stood in front of it, and four behind. But almost all those seats were empty.

The girls sat on one side of the room and the boys on the other. Mary Power and Minnie Johnson shared one of the back seats on the girls' side.

Cap Garland and three other big boys sat in back seats on the boys' side. In the front seats were a few little boys and girls.

Laura and Carrie didn't know where to sit.

"You're new, aren't you?" asked Teacher. She was a smiling young lady. Her dress was buttoned with shiny black buttons.

Laura told her their names.

"And I'm Florence Garland," said Teacher.

"We live in back of your father's place, on the next street."

So Cap Garland was Teacher's brother. Laura knew their house. She had seen it from the attic window at home.

"Do you know the Fourth Reader?" Teacher asked.

"Oh, yes, ma'am!" Laura said. She did indeed know every word of it.

"Then I think we'll see what you can do with the Fifth," said Teacher. She told Laura to take the back seat in the middle row, across the aisle from Mary Power.

Carrie was told to sit in front, near the little girls. Then Teacher went up to her desk and rapped on it with her ruler.

"The school will come to attention," she said. Everyone took out their books. School had begun.

Every day Laura liked school more. She

made friends with Mary Power and Minnie Johnson. They sat together at recess and ate together at noon. By the end of the week they were meeting in the mornings and walking together to school.

The boys who sat with Cap Garland were named Ben Woodworth and Arthur Johnson. Ben was a brown-eyed, dark-haired boy. He lived at the depot. Arthur was Minnie's brother. He looked a lot like her, thin and fair.

But Cap Garland was the strongest boy, and the quickest. He was not as handsome as Ben, but there was something about him. His grin was like a flash of light. It made you happy to see him smile.

Mary Power and Minnie and Cap had all gone to schools in the East. But Laura found it easy to keep up with them. Even in arithmetic Cap Garland could not beat Laura.

Laura decided she liked this new school.

In fact, she was enjoying it so much that she was sorry when Saturday came. She looked forward to Monday, when she could go back to school.

CHAPTER 8
THE BLIZZARD

But when Monday came Laura was cross. Ma said she had to wear her red flannel underwear. Laura hated it. It was hot and scratchy. It made her back itch like crazy. Her neck itched, and so did her wrists and ankles.

At noon she begged Ma to let her change. "It's too hot for my red flannels, Ma!"

But Ma was firm. "I know the weather's turned warm. But this is the time of year to wear flannels. You could catch cold if you took them off."

Laura went back to school, feeling grumpy. She sat squirming at her desk. She must not scratch. But the itching flannels were all she could think about. She tried to study, but she couldn't concentrate.

Itch, itch, itch. The afternoon dragged by. The sunshine from the western windows had never crawled so slowly.

Then, suddenly, there was no sunshine at all. It was as if someone had blown out the sun like a lamp.

Outside it was gray. Wind crashed against the schoolhouse, shaking the walls. The windows rattled. One of the little girls screamed. Teacher jumped up from her chair.

Laura's heart thumped. She remembered once when Pa had been lost in a blizzard, back on Plum Creek. That terrible storm had started just like this.

Teacher and all the others were staring at the windows. But there was nothing to see, just thick snow whirling down. The children were frightened.

"It is only a storm," said Teacher. "Go on with your lessons."

The wind crashed and moaned against the walls. The sounds of the blizzard grew louder and louder.

Laura bent her head over her books. But she was not studying. She tried to think how to get home. The schoolhouse was a long way from Main Street. There was nothing in between to guide them.

Laura knew they could easily get lost in a blizzard like this. The flying snow made it impossible to see. They might wander in the wrong direction and get lost out on the open prairie.

But if they stayed at school, they might freeze to death. There was only a little coal to burn in the stove. Laura knew they'd have to burn the expensive desks for firewood. Even then they might not have enough fuel to keep from freezing.

Laura looked up at Teacher. She was biting her lip and thinking. Laura knew Teacher had never seen a storm like this. She, like all the others, had moved there from the East last summer. None of them had lived through a prairie blizzard.

But Laura and Carrie had. Laura could see that Carrie was scared. Laura was scared too.

She could see that Teacher was trying to decide what to do. She couldn't dismiss school because of a storm, but this storm frightened her.

"I ought to tell her what to do," Laura thought. But she didn't know what to say. It was not safe to leave the schoolhouse. And it was not safe to stay. The room was already growing colder.

Laura jumped. Someone was thumping in the entry. Everyone looked at the door.

A man stumbled in. He was all white, covered with snow. His scarf was stiff with ice. They could not see who he was until he pulled the scarf away from his face.

It was Mr. Foster, who lived across the street from Teacher. "I came out to get you," he said.

Teacher thanked him. She rapped her ruler on the desk. "Attention! School is dismissed."

Everyone went for their coats and hoods. The entry was freezing cold, so they huddled around the stove to get dressed. Snow was beginning to blow through cracks in the walls.

Laura took hold of Carrie's mittened hand. "Don't worry," she told her sister. "We'll be all right."

"Now, just follow me," said Mr. Foster. "And keep close together."

He and Teacher led the way out the door into the blinding snow. The wind was blowing so hard Laura could hardly walk. After just a few steps she could no longer see the schoolhouse. All she could see was whirling, swirling whiteness.

Laura gripped Carrie's hand tightly. Ice stung her face. The wind whipped her skirts around her feet, nearly tripping her. It was even worse for Carrie. The wind shoved her against Laura, then pulled her away.

"We can't go on this way," Laura thought. But they had to.

It seemed as though they stumbled through the snow forever. Laura began to worry. She couldn't see any of the other students ahead or Teacher or Mr. Foster. She must walk faster and keep up with them or she and Carrie would be lost. If they were lost on the prairie they would freeze to death.

The storm thinned a little. Laura could see shadowy figures ahead. She hurried to catch up, pulling Carrie along. They reached Teacher, who had stopped walking.

Everyone had stopped in a huddle. Teacher and Mr. Foster were trying to talk, but the wind carried their voices away.

Laura shook with cold. She was afraid for Carrie. The cold hurt too much. Carrie could not stand it for long. They must reach shelter soon.

Main Street was only two blocks long. It seemed to Laura that they should have reached the stores by now. If they got off track, if they missed Main Street, they could wander out onto the open prairie and be lost.

Mr. Foster and Teacher were moving again, going a little to the left. Laura and Carrie hurried along. Then a shadow passed Laura, going straight ahead. It was Cap Garland. He was not following the others.

Laura did not dare follow him. She must stay with Teacher. But Laura had a feeling that Cap was going toward Main Street. If he was right, then Teacher and Mr. Foster were wrong. They would all be lost.

They trudged on and on in the dizzying snow. Carrie was tired. Laura knew Carrie wouldn't be able to go much farther. But she was too heavy for Laura to carry. They must go on as long as they could.

Then something smacked against Laura. She rocked on her feet. It was the corner of a building.

With all her might she yelled, "Here!

Come here! Here's a house!"

At first no one heard her. She screamed and screamed. At last she saw a shadow, and another, and another. They crowded around her. Everyone was there—Teacher, Mr. Foster, Mary Power and Minnie, Ben and Arthur, and the other students.

Only Cap Garland was missing.

They followed the wall until they came to the front of the building. It was Mead's Hotel. It was the last building on Main Street. If they had missed it, they would have been lost on the endless prairie.

Minnie and Arthur Johnson lived right across Main Street from the hotel. The others went on down the street, keeping close to the buildings. One by one, the students reached their homes.

At last Laura saw a lighted window that was her very own house. She and Carrie were safe at home. Pa opened the door and helped them in.

He was wearing his overcoat. "I was just starting out after you," he said.

Laura and Carrie stood in the still house taking deep breaths. It was so quiet there where the winds did not push and pull at them.

Laura felt Ma's hands breaking away her icy scarf. "Is Carrie all right?" she asked.

"Yes, Carrie's all right," said Pa.

Ma helped them take off their coats. Ice crackled and fell to the floor. "Well," Ma said. "All's well that ends well. You're not frostbitten. You can go to the fire and get warm."

Pa took Carrie on his knee, holding her close to the stove. She was shivering. "I can't get warm, Pa," she said.

"I'll get you a hot drink," said Ma. She hurried into the kitchen and came out with two steaming cups of ginger tea.

"My, that smells good!" said Mary.

It was so wonderful to be safe at home. Laura sipped the hot, sweet ginger tea. Slowly she grew warm and comfortable.

"I'm glad you didn't have to come for us, Pa," she said.

"So am I," said Carrie. "I remembered that Christmas, on Plum Creek, when you didn't get home."

"I did, too," Pa said grimly. "When Cap Garland came into Fuller's and said you were all heading out to the open prairie, you can bet I made tracks for a rope and lantern. Cap Garland's a smart boy."

So Cap had been right. Laura was glad he had made it safely home, too.

"And now, Laura and Carrie, you're going to bed and get some rest," said Ma. "A good long sleep is what you need."

CHAPTER 9
STUDYING AT HOME

School was closed the next day and the next while the blizzard raged on. It was only the first of many blizzards that long, hard winter. Sometimes there was no school for weeks on end.

But every day Laura found time to study a little. She spread her books out on the table, with Mary beside her. Laura read the arithmetic problems out loud, and Mary did them in her head while Laura worked them on the slate. She read the history and geography lessons to Mary until both of them could answer every question.

Perhaps one day Pa would save up enough money to send Mary to the college for the blind. Mary must be ready to go, just in case.

"And even if I never can go to college," Mary said, "I'm learning as much as I can."

The long, dark winter dragged on and on. One terrible day, the supply of coal ran out. Pa had to think of another way to keep the fire going or they would all freeze. There was plenty of hay, but it burned up too fast.

Then Pa thought of twisting handfuls of hay into hard, tight sticks. It burned more slowly that way.

"Sticks of hay!" Ma laughed. "What won't you think of next? Trust you, Charles, to find a way."

One evening, when Laura had helped

twist enough hay to last for an hour, she sat down to study. But she felt dull and stupid. She could not remember history or geography. She leaned her head on her hand and stared at her slate.

"Come, come, girls! We must not mope," said Ma. "Straighten up, Laura and Carrie! Do your lessons briskly and then we'll have an entertainment."

"How, Ma?" Carrie asked.

"Get your lessons first," said Ma.

When studytime was over, Ma took the Fifth Reader. "Now," she said, "let's see how much you can repeat from memory. You first, Mary. What shall it be?"

"The Speech of Regulus," said Mary. Ma opened the book to the right page.

Mary began. "'Ye doubtless thought—for ye judge of Roman virtue by your own—that I would break my plighted oath rather than,

returning, brook your vengeance!'" Mary knew the whole speech by heart. Laura and Carrie listened proudly. The small kitchen seemed to grow larger and warmer as Mary spoke the splendid words.

"You did that perfectly, Mary," Ma said.

Then it was Laura's turn. She chose a poem called "Old Tubal Cain." The verses lifted her to her feet. Her voice rang out:

"Old Tubal Cain was a man of might,
In the days when the earth was young.
By the fierce red light of his furnace bright,
The strokes of his hammer rung . . ."

Pa came in before Laura reached the end. "Go on, go on," he said. "That warms me as much as the fire."

So Laura went on, while Pa leaned over the fire to melt the ice from his eyebrows.

"And sang, 'Hurrah for Tubal Cain!
Our staunch good friend is he;
And for the plowshare and the plow
To him our praise shall be . . .'"

When she finished, Ma congratulated her. "You remembered every word correctly, Laura." Ma closed the book. "Carrie and Grace shall have their turns tomorrow."

Then it was time to twist more hay. The sharp stuff cut Laura's hands and it was shivering cold out in the lean-to, but tonight Laura didn't mind. The wonderful words of the poem echoed in her head.

After that, afternoons were something to look forward to. The Fifth Reader was full of beautiful speeches and poems. Mary knew many of them by heart, and Laura was eager to learn them. She and Mary and Carrie took turns reciting. Even little Grace knew

"Mary's Little Lamb," and "Bo-peep Has Lost Her Sheep."

Grace's blue eyes shone with excitement when Laura chanted:

"Listen, my children, and you shall hear
Of the midnight ride of Paul Revere.
The eighteenth of April in Seventy-five,
Hardly a man is now alive
Who remembers that famous day and
year . . ."

Then there was a poem called "The Swan's Nest," that Laura and Carrie loved to recite together:

"Little Ellie sits alone
'Mid the beeches of a meadow,
By a stream side, on the grass,
And the trees are showering down

Doubles of their leaves in shadow
On her shining hair and face . . ."

When Laura and Carrie spoke those words they forgot about the snow beating on the walls outside. They hardly heard the icy blizzard winds. They were in a green meadow where the air was warm and quiet.

One Sunday Ma suggested a Bible verse contest. "Mary, you tell us a verse, then Laura will do the same, and then Carrie. See which one can keep on longest."

"Oh, Mary will win," Carrie said.

"Come on! I'll help you," Laura urged.

"Two against one isn't fair," Mary objected.

"It is too fair!" Laura said. "Isn't it, Ma? When Mary's been learning Bible verses so much longer than Carrie has."

"Yes," Ma decided. "But Laura must only prompt Carrie."

Mary began. They went on and on until Carrie couldn't remember any more verses. Then Mary and Laura went on against each other.

At last Laura had to give up. She hated to admit that she was beaten, but she had to. "You beat me, Mary. I can't remember another one."

"Mary beat! Mary beat!" Grace cried, clapping her hands.

Ma smiled at Mary. "That's my bright girl."

They all looked at Mary. Her beautiful blue eyes that couldn't see were bright with joy. For a minute she looked as she used to look when she could see.

Then she blushed pink. In a low voice she said, "I didn't beat you, Laura. We're even. I can't remember another verse, either."

Laura was ashamed. She had tried so hard

to beat Mary at this game. But no matter how hard she tried, she could never be as good as Mary. Mary was truly good.

Suddenly Laura knew what she wanted to do. She wanted to become a schoolteacher. If she taught school, she could save enough money to send Mary to college.

She knew that Mary wanted to go to college more than anything. "There's so much to learn," Mary always said. "And to think that I can, if we can save the money, even now that I'm blind. Isn't it wonderful?"

Laura agreed. It was wonderful. And she could make sure Mary got the chance to go. Someday, Laura decided, she would teach in a little schoolhouse just like Miss Beadle and Miss Garland and Ma.

And she did.

If you're done with your chores,
have fun with these

activities!

Meet Laura

The Little House Family Tree

Word Scramble

Word Search

Sing-Along: "Uncle John"

A Special Look at *Laura & Nellie*,
a Little House Chapter Book

MEET LAURA

Laura Ingalls Wilder was born in the Big Woods of Wisconsin on February 7, 1867, to Charles Ingalls and his wife, Caroline.

When Laura was still a baby, Pa and Ma decided to move to a farm near Keytesville, Missouri, and the family lived there about a year. Then they moved to land on the prairie south of Independence, Kansas. After two years in their little house on the prairie, the Ingallses went back to the Big Woods to live in the same house they had left three years earlier.

This time the family remained in the Big Woods for three years. These were the years that Laura wrote about in her first book, *Little House in the Big Woods.*

In the winter of 1874, when Laura was seven, Ma and Pa decided to move west to Minnesota. They found a beautiful farm near Walnut Grove, on the banks of Plum Creek.

The next two years were hard ones for the Ingallses. Swarms of grasshoppers devoured all the crops in the area, and Ma and Pa could not pay off all their debts. The family decided they could no longer keep the farm on Plum Creek, so they moved to Burr Oak, Iowa.

After a year in Iowa, the family returned to Walnut Grove again, and Pa built a house in town and started a butcher shop. Laura was ten years old by then, and she helped earn money for the family by working in the dining room of the hotel in Walnut Grove, babysitting, and running errands.

The family moved only once more, to the little town of De Smet in Dakota Territory. Laura was now twelve and had lived in at least twelve little houses. Laura grew into a young lady in De Smet, and met her husband, Almanzo Wilder, there.

Laura and Almanzo were married in 1885, and their daughter, Rose, was born in December 1886. By the spring of 1890, Laura and Almanzo had endured too many hardships to continue farming in South Dakota. Their house had burned down in 1889, and their second child, a boy, had died before he was a month old.

First, Laura, Almanzo, and Rose went east to Spring Valley, Minnesota, to live with Almanzo's family. About a year later they moved south to Florida. But Laura did not like Florida, and the family returned to De Smet.

In 1894, Laura, Almanzo, and Rose left De Smet for good and settled in Mansfield, Missouri.

When Laura was in her fifties, she began to write down her memories of her childhood, and in 1932, when Laura was 65 years old, *Little House in the Big Woods* was published. It was an immediate success, and Laura was asked to write more books about her life on the frontier.

Laura died on February 10, 1957, three days after her ninetieth birthday, but interest in the Little House books continued to grow. Since their first publication so many years ago, the Little House books have been read by millions of readers all over the world.

The Little House Family Tree

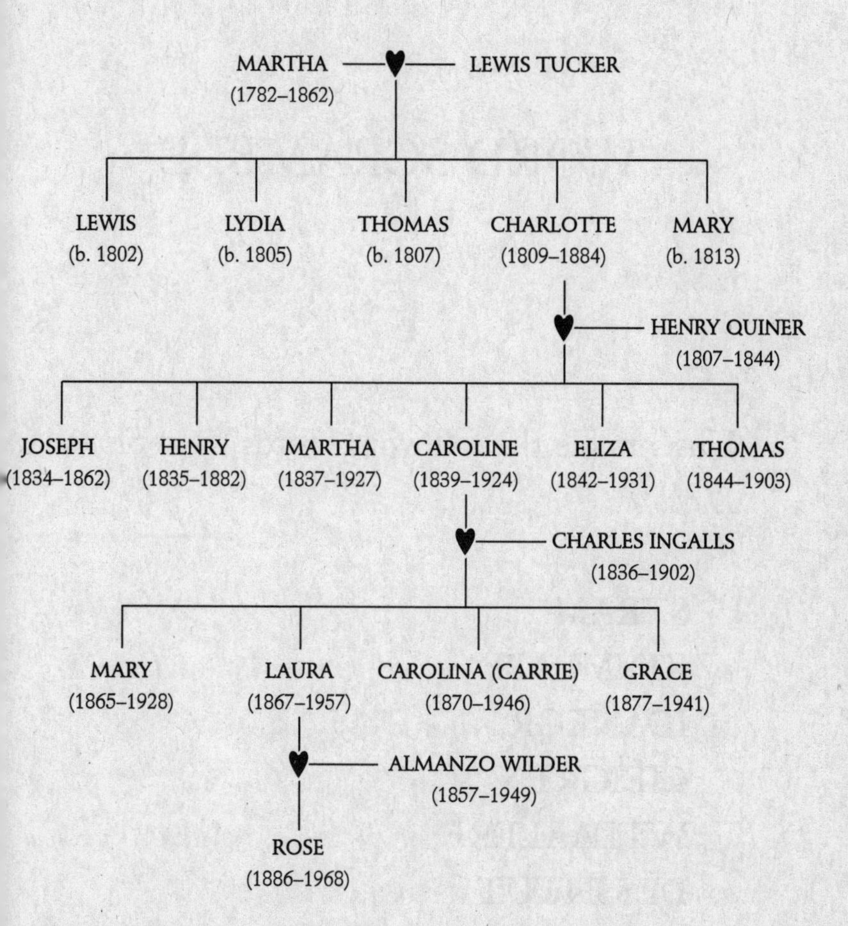

WORD SCRAMBLE

Unscramble the following words from *School Days*!

STRAM
KINMLABL
IDANEGR
CIEIGRTN
WTLAALERF
DESSNTUT
ITWER

FTNLAKUH

SBUTNNOEN

YMREUBDARL

SUBIGILDN

IHABSTKCML

GLRAADN

ISSNEP

KECLSRFE

EINELL

TCNRYUO

SKEDS

DLEABE

UHOOECHSOSL

WORD SEARCH

Find the following words from *School Days* in the puzzle below!

TEACHER	PLAYING	HALF-PINT
BENCH	DANCING	GEOGRAPHY
SLATE	SURPRISE	LESSONS
BELL	BOOKS	HISTORY
PENCIL	ARITHMETIC	POEM
CANDY	STUDYING	SPEECH
HANDSOME	SCHOOL	

S E G E O G R A P H Y S H
T A C B F I B K O J P C I
U H A N D S O M E E H H S
D P N J M Q O A M H Q O T
Y O D X E F K U B A P O O
I M Y A J Q S S H L L L R
N L B P I B E L L F A B Y
G P S H T U N S A P Y M A
Q E U B E N C H E I I F R
G N T S A L H O X N N S I
S C F C C X Y O I T G L T
N I M A H R X G U N R E H
S L A T E U P T C I Q S M
O R G Q R S U R P R I S E
P A S N O S H J N S T O T
D A N C I N G S R A G N I
Q C H R S P E E C H T S C

ANSWER KEY

Word Scramble:

SMART	SUNBONNET
MILLBANK	LUMBERYARD
READING	BUILDINGS
RECITING	BLACKSMITH
WATERFALL	GARLAND
STUDENTS	SNIPES
WRITE	FRECKLES
THANKFUL	NELLIE

COUNTRY

DESKS

BEADLE

SCHOOLHOUSE

Word Search:

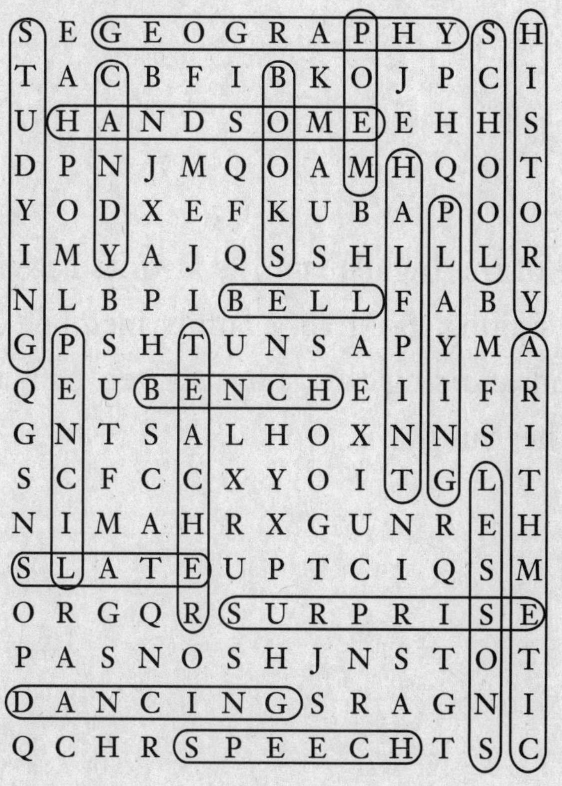

SING-ALONG

One of the Ingalls family's favorite activities was singing. So grab a family member or a friend and sing this song beloved by Laura and her family!

"Uncle John"

Uncle John is a singing game, following the tune of "Yankee Doodle." Here's how you play:

1. The players walk in a circle while singing the first two verses of "Uncle John."

2. At the end of the second verse the players sit down as fast as they can.

3. The last one to sit goes to the center of the circle and gives the name of a favorite person.

4. The players start walking in a circle again, singing the third verse of the song using the name of the person in the center of the circle and his or her friend's name to fill in the blanks.

5. At the end of the song, all the players dance around, and then come back to a circle, ready to play again.

(Note: The lyrics of the third verse can be adjusted, depending on whether it's a boy or girl in the circle.)

Uncle John is sick in bed,
What shall we send him?
A piece of pie, a piece of cake,
A piece of apple dumpling.
What shall we send it in?
In a piece of paper.
Paper is not fine enough;

In a golden saucer.

Uncle John is sick in bed,
What shall we send him?
A piece of pie, a piece of cake,
A piece of apple dumpling.
Who shall we send it by?
By the governor's daughter.
Take her by the lily-white hand,
And lead her o'er the water.

[Name of person in circle] so they say,
Goes acourting night and day,
Sword and pistol by his side,
And [name of friend] to be his bride.
Takes her by the lily-white hand,
And leads her o'er the water.
Here's a kiss, and there's a kiss,
For Mr. [last name of friend]'s daughter.

Laura and her sisters may live in a little house, but they're always ready for big adventure. Don't miss:

CHAPTER 1
COUNTRY GIRLS

Laura Ingalls never forgot the first time she met Nellie Oleson. It was on Laura's first day of school, when she lived in Minnesota.

Laura and her big sister, Mary, and her little sister, Carrie, lived on a farm with their Ma and Pa and their bulldog, Jack. Living on a farm meant Laura was a country girl.

Laura loved being a country girl. She loved to run out of the house in the morning and see the dew sparkling on the prairie grass.

She loved to wade in the creek where the minnows swam. She loved to poke a stick at the old crab who lived in the creek and watch him come out snapping his sharp claws. She loved the good smells of hay and earth and wind.

Nellie Oleson was not a country girl. She was a town girl.

When Nellie Oleson first saw Laura, she wrinkled up her nose as though she smelled something bad. She didn't—she was just being snooty. Nellie's father owned a store, and Nellie thought that made her very important.

"Hmph!" sniffed Nellie Oleson, looking Laura and Mary up and down. She looked at their faded dresses and their long legs sticking out from under the hems. She looked at their braids, tied with thread.

"Country girls!" she said.

Laura didn't much like Nellie Oleson,

even if she did have pretty yellow curls tied with big blue ribbons. Nellie's dress was store-bought. It was smooth and white, with little blue flowers all over. Nellie wore shiny black shoes, and her dress was as light and delicate as a spring day. She was pretty as a picture, except for that wrinkled-up nose.

Laura and Mary were barefoot. When the weather was warm, they always went barefoot. They loved the feel of the soft grass and warm dirt beneath their feet. Ma made all their clothes. She bought sturdy red calico for Laura's dresses, and sturdy blue calico for Mary's. Laura and Mary had never had a white dress like Nellie's.

But Laura and Mary were too busy that first day of school to worry much about Nellie Oleson. They had never been to school before, even though Laura was almost eight and Mary was going on nine. Until now, the places they had lived in had been too far away from any town for them to go to school.

They were excited to meet their teacher, Miss Beadle. She let them inside the one-room schoolhouse and showed them where to sit.

Ma had given Laura and Mary a book to study from. But they did not have a slate.

"I will lend you mine," Teacher said. "You cannot learn to write without a slate."

She lifted up the top of her desk and took out a piece of black board. That was the slate. There was a piece of chalk, too, to write on the slate with.

At noon, all the other children went home to eat. Laura and Mary's house on the farm was two and a half miles away. That was too long a walk to go home for dinner. So Laura and Mary took their dinner pail and sat in a shady spot against the schoolhouse. They ate their bread and butter and talked.

"I like school," Mary said.

"So do I," said Laura. "But I don't like that Nellie Oleson that called us country girls."

"We are country girls," Mary pointed out.

"Yes," Laura said proudly. "She needn't wrinkle her nose!"

CHAPTER 2
TOWN GIRL

The very next day, Laura and Mary had to go to Nellie's father's store. Pa had given them a nickel to buy a slate of their own. They must not go on borrowing Teacher's slate, he said.

The morning sun was shining brightly when they climbed the steps of Mr. Oleson's store. Laura blinked a little inside the cool shady building.

A man stood behind the counter. Laura guessed that was Mr. Oleson, the shopkeeper.

She looked around at all the wonderful things on the shelves—pails and pickles and ploughs and a large round yellow cheese. There were dozens of interesting things for sale. Laura would have liked to look at them all.

But suddenly the back door slammed open. In flounced Nellie Oleson. She looked right at Laura and Mary, standing in the doorway in their bare feet.

"Yah! Yah!" shouted a little boy behind Nellie. He was her brother, Willie, and he had teased Laura and Mary at school the day before. He had called them snipes because their dresses were too short. Snipes were birds with funny long legs, and Laura and Mary did look a little like snipes with their legs sticking out beneath the hems of their dresses. But it wasn't nice to be reminded of it.

"Yah! Long-legged snipes!" Willie jeered now.

"Shut up, Willie," said Mr. Oleson.

But Willie did not shut up. He went on saying, "Snipes! Snipes!"

With a little smile on her face, Nellie walked right past Mary and Laura to a tall wooden barrel that stood on the floor. She dug her hands into the pail and came up with two fistfuls of candy.

It was Christmas candy. There were striped pieces, round pieces, pieces like ribbons. There was red and green and white candy. It was beautiful! Nellie stared right at Laura and Mary, as she crammed the beautiful candies into her mouth.

Willie laughed, and grabbed a handful of candy for himself. He shoveled it into his mouth. Neither one of them offered any to Laura or Mary. Not a single piece.

"Nellie! You and Willie go right back out of here!" Mr. Oleson said.

But Nellie and Willie ignored him. *Crunch, crunch* went the candy in their mouths. They kept on staring at Mary and Laura.

Mary turned away from them. She told Mr. Oleson she needed a slate and handed him Pa's nickel.

Mr. Oleson gave her the slate. "You'll want a slate pencil, too," he said. "Here it is. One penny."

"They haven't got a penny," Nellie said.

"Well, take it along, and tell your Pa to give me the penny next time he comes to town," said Mr. Oleson.

But Mary said, "No, sir. Thank you." She turned around and so did Laura, and they walked out of the store.

At the door Laura looked back. Nellie made a face at her. Nellie's tongue was streaked red and green from the candy.

Laura and Mary were quiet as they walked

to the schoolhouse. Laura was worried about the slate pencil they needed to buy. She hated to ask Pa for another penny, after he had spent so much on the slate. Then she remembered their Christmas pennies. One year, back in Indian Territory, they had each found a penny in their Christmas stockings. They could use those pennies for slate pencils. And they would buy the pencils at Mr. Beadle's store, not at Mr. Oleson's.

That made Laura feel better. But she kept thinking about Nellie sticking out her red-and-green tongue.

Mary was still thinking about Nellie, too. "My goodness!" she said. "I couldn't be as mean as that Nellie Oleson."

I could, Laura thought. I could be meaner to her than she is to us, if Ma and Pa would let me.